Bedtime

Hullabaloo

Bedtime Hullabaloo

First published in Great Britain in 2010 by Hodder Children's Books
First published in the United States of America in October 2010 by
Walker Publishing Company, Inc., a division of Bloomsbury Publishing, Inc.
Visit Walker & Company's Web site at www.bloomsburykids.com

For information about permission to reproduce selections from this book, write to
Permissions, Walker & Company, 175 Fifth Avenue, New York, New York 10010

Library of Congress Cataloging-in-Publication Data
Conway, David, 1970-
Bedtime hullabaloo / David Conway ; illustrated by Charles Fuge.
p.   cm.
Summary: One night in the silly savannah as some animals are preparing for bed, they are disturbed by a loud
hubbub and set out to discover its source.
ISBN 978-0-8027-2170-9
[1. Savannah animals—Fiction. 2. Animal sounds—Fiction. 3. Noise—Fiction.] I. Fuge, Charles, ill. II. Title.
PZ7.C76835Be 2010   [E]—dc22   2009038964

Printed in China by WKT Company Ltd., Shenzhen, Guangdong
2 4 6 8 10 9 7 5 3 1

DAVID CONWAY   illustrated by CHARLES FUGE

Bedtime
Hullabaloo

Walker & Company   New York

ONE NIGHT ON THE SILLY SAVANNAH,

a ludicrous leopard was leapfrogging to bed when all
of a sudden there was a terrible racket…

"What a hullabaloo!" said the leopard
and decided to follow the noise.

Along the way, the leopard passed
by a sleepy giraffe singing a
lullaby when all of a sudden...

HHHRRR-ZZZ!

SNORT, SNORT!

"What a hullabaloo!" said the giraffe
and decided to follow the noise.

The leopard and
the giraffe then met a
baboon who was reading
a bedtime story to the moon
when all of a sudden...

HHHRRR-ZZZ!

SNORT, SNORT!

GRUNT, GRUNT!

"What a hullabaloo!"
said the baboon and decided
to follow the noise.

The three animals followed the noise
to check out all the fuss and discover
the source of this bedtime din, this
clamor, this hubbub, this rumpus.

Under the still, starlit night they walked.
The noise began to swell.

More and more animals joined in the search
to seek out the nuisance as well. There was
a hat-wearing hyena half-asleep, a music-making
meerkat counting sheep…

... a zany zebra who was having a dream
about sailing upon a sea of ice cream,

a sleepwalking lion with bedraggled hair,
an outraged ostrich clutching a teddy bear,
and a polka-dot-pajama-wearing water buffalo.

So on they walked all into the night, all sleepy and
tired and very uptight. Through the long giggling

grass, past the tickling tree, and when they came

Not a raucous
rhinoceros…

or a cacophonous
hippopotamus…

an ear-splitting
elephant...

or a crazy monkey...

…but a tiny shrew, wearing a pink tutu, snoring its head off very loudly.

HHHRRR-ZZZ!

SNORT, SNORT! GRUNT, GRUNT!

Something had to be done. Leopard growled as loud as it could. Giraffe bleated even louder.

Baboon screeched with
all its might until…

...the terrible
racket woke
the shrew from
its thunderous
slumber.

And all was quiet on the silly savannah once more,
so quiet you couldn't hear a peep…

...until the silence was suddenly shattered
by some animals fast asleep in a heap.

R-ZZZ!

SNORT,
SNORT!

GRUNT,
GRUNT!

SNUFFLE,
SNUFFLE!

BUT NOT FOR LONG!